BJARKI THE VIKING

J. DICKMAN

For Mum, Dad and Nana

First Published 2010 by Appin Press, an imprint of Countyvise Ltd.
14 Appin Road, Birkenhead, CH41 9HH

Copyright © 2010 J. Dickman

The right of J. Dickman to be identified as the author of this work has been asserted by her in accordance with the Copyright, Design and Patents Act 1988.

British Library Cataloguing in Publication Data.
A catalogue record for this book is available from the British Library.

ISBN 978 1 906205 46 1

THANKS

Special thanks go to Mandy for her support in making me believe I could write a story and also for proof reading, feedback and being the first of a select few to read it. Thanks too for feedback from my 'bestest' friend, Liz, and also to my Dad and Julie. Many thanks also to Sarah, who has done an excellent job on all the drawings and front cover especially given the 'stickmen' sketches I provided! The map of Bjarki's world is however mine.

ABOUT THE AUTHOR

 J. Dickman was born on the Wirral but now lives in Lancashire. She still has strong family ties with the Wirral and visits regularly. She has travelled extensively in Scandinavia and goes back at any and every opportunity, especially to Sweden. She says 'I was born on the Wirral but my home is Sweden'. She has always had a strong

pull toward Scandinavia and the Viking heritage of the Wirral. On her first visit to Birka she felt a spooky feeling of déjà vu.

Her opportunity to write this book that she first had the idea for in 2006 arose from being made redundant. 'Bjarki' encompasses many of her real interests - history, geography, place names and Scandinavia - interests which go back to when she was a child. It is her first book, though she has had articles published in professional journals on surveying and town planning as well as travel articles on Sweden and Norway.

She is a chartered surveyor and chartered town planner and now runs her own town planning consultancy in NW England. Her other business ventures have a Scandinavian theme – calendars, travel writing and bespoke canvas prints.

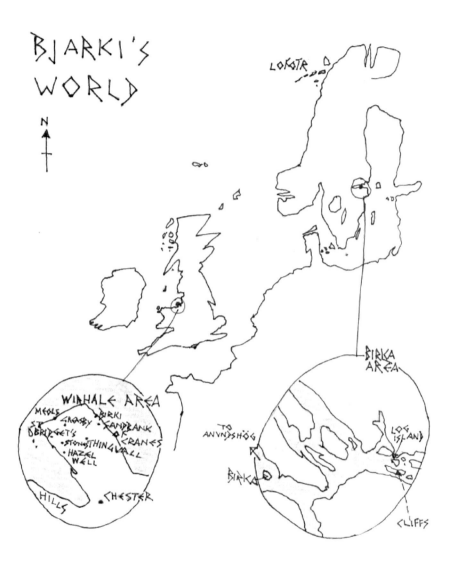

PROLOGUE

It was a fairly non-eventful day in Asgard. The gods were sitting around in the summer sunshine playing games and chatting. Summer in Asgard was sunshine 24/7. Frigg and Sif were having a girly chat about the latest fashions in Asgard. Odin was scanning the other worlds just to check nothing was happening that he needed to deal with. Balder was admiring himself in the mirror – one of his favourite pastimes.

All of a sudden Balder put the mirror down and looked around.

'Where's Loki?' Balder asked. He'd never trusted Loki, always sly and underhand.

'I have no idea sweetie,' replied Frigg, smiling at her blond blue-eyed son.

Balder was very, very handsome and all the other goddesses, the Valkyries and human women swooned after him, but his mother treated him no different than his siblings.

'I think you're getting a bit paranoid about

Loki, my dear,' said Frigg, patting his arm. 'There's no need to worry about him.'

'What's going on?'

It was the sonorous booming voice of Odin, the chief god. He had given one of his eyes to Mimir to gain knowledge and be all knowing. His remaining eye could see everything so as well as scanning the other worlds he was keeping a close eye on his immediate surroundings. Now he looked directly at his wife and son.

'What's going on?' he repeated.

'Nothing dear,' replied Frigg, casting him a quick glance.

'I thought I heard Balder whining again about Loki. He's just beauty and no brains that lad. People think he'll come good one day, but he'll be the death of us all, you mark my words.' Odin frowned at Balder who was pointedly looking away. Then he sighed. 'Tell you what, there's not much happening today. Why don't we play I spy? You know, I spy with my all seeing eye......everything! Ha ha ha!' Odin chortled loudly at his own joke.

Frigg shrugged her shoulders, rolled her eyes and tutted. 'Yes dear, very droll.'

'The old ones are the best,' chuckled Odin.

'Whatever you say dear,' replied Frigg.

Suddenly the ground started to shake. Thud! Thud! Thud! The heavy footsteps came nearer.

'Thor is on his way home,' said his wife, Sif, 'and he doesn't sound very happy.'

Frigg shook her head, knowing the ways of her stepson all too well.

The ground continued to shake as Thor stomped into view. Looking at Thor and Balder you'd never believe they were brothers. Thor was a huge giant of a man with a voice more booming and deeper than Odin's. As the god of thunder, a fact he liked everyone to know, but frankly it didn't take much guessing, he liked to cause storms and throw lightning bolts using his hammer, Mjolnir, which was like a boomerang and always came back to Thor. Now he held an empty hand up to the sky.

'Someone has stolen my hammer,' roared Thor. Everyone held their breath - they knew it was unwise to get in Thor's way when he was angry. They were relieved when he stomped over to Odin.

'Dad, can you see if you can see it anywhere please?' he asked Odin. 'I bet it's Loki.'

Balder nodded eagerly in agreement from behind his mother.

'Yes that little slimy toad, he's up to his tricks again.'

'What's he done to you?' Thor asked.

'I just don't trust him,' replied Balder quietly, looking down.

Thor shook his head and looked at Odin again.

'Dad, please will you have a look at Earth and the other worlds and see if you can see Mjolnir?' pleaded Thor.

Odin was sure Thor had just mislaid Mjolnir, but he nodded and peered through the clouds.

'It's all pretty quiet in the other worlds,' commented Odin. 'Nothing much going on. Oh hang on a sec - will you look at that?'

'What is it? You've found Mjolnir?' asked Thor eagerly.

'No. Frigg, come and look.'

His wife came over and peered over his shoulder through the clouds to where Odin was pointing. 'Odin, I think you're going soppy in your old age, it's only a wedding.'

Odin's eye twinkled. 'I was remembering ours. I was on Cloud 9 when you agreed to marry me and we had such a lovely day here in Asgard. You looked so beautiful in your flowing white dress with gold and silver threads running through it shimmering in the sunlight.'

Frigg smiled and asked, 'So whose wedding is it that we're nosing in on?'

'Some guy called Erik from Birka,' said Odin. 'He's on Lofotr, marrying his best friend's sister, Signy. Looks like he's done well for himself. That guy must be very wealthy to attract a wife like that.'

Sif joined them and looked at the wedding scene too. She gasped.

'Signy is stunning. I really like her dress. Very expensive. I think the off-white colour with the blue trimmings really suits her, with her long red hair. And wow - Erik is very handsome!' said Sif, catching a closer look at the groom.

Balder, who so far had shown no interest in the matter, suddenly looked up.

'Who's handsome?' asked Balder

Frigg smiled. 'Well the groom is good looking, but he's not as handsome as you, sweetie,' she said, before Balder got all upset.

'Oh for goodness sake!' boomed Thor, getting mad. 'Who cares about a flippin' wedding, or offending Pretty Boy here!' Thor jabbed his thumb in Balder's direction. 'I asked if you could see my hammer, Dad.'

'No, I can't son,' replied Odin

Thor's face slowly turned red, his eyes ablaze

as he grabbed the first couple of things he could lay his hands on, namely two huge red boulders each the size of a house and threw them as far as he could. As they landed the earth shook.

*****

Down on Lofotr the day was full of merriment. Signy and Erik's wedding was a cause for great celebration. There was loads of ale and mead to drink and tons of wild boar and herring to eat.

'Skål,' shouted Olaf toasting his sister and best friend, with his arms draped over the shoulders of the wedding couple. 'Cheers, a toast to the happy couple. Don't they make a beautiful match?' He gave Signy a kiss on the cheek and slapped Erik good naturedly on the back. Everyone cheered. This wedding was important. Finally, the chieftains of the Norwegian and Swedish Vikings were now family.

The music started up, and Erik and Signy got up to dance. Soon the guests joined them on the dance floor. The band, a local one called Fest, were friends of Signy's – in fact, she used to be their lead singer. She loved to sing and had a hauntingly beautiful voice, but moving to Birka with Erik meant giving it up. After a few songs the new lead singer called to Signy and said 'Come on, give us a tune for old times sake!' She laughed and shook her head, holding on to Erik as the rest of the band came over. They were all laughing together as they hauled her up onto the stage. As she started singing the room fell silent - her voice mesmerised the crowd. They couldn't get enough of her - the singing and dancing went on and on into the night. No one really noticed, because on Lofotr in the summer the sun never sets, being north of the Arctic Circle.

As the party drew to a close Erik and Signy slipped away down to the waterside where all the longships were moored. The ships were a stunning sight as the reddish golden glow of the big yellowy orange sun dipped to touch the top of the horizon. The sea looked and moved more like mercury than water and had that same silvery look to it. The huge spiky mountains were silhouetted against the low sun and looked close enough to touch. Soon they'd be setting off for Birka. Erik stood with his arm round his new wife and pointed out his longship.

Erik was still gobsmacked that Signy had agreed to marry him and return with him to

Birka. It would be a long journey and once there, she wouldn't know anyone apart from Erik. But she was an outgoing, friendly type and Erik knew she would soon win people over. He couldn't wait to start his new life with her and have a family: his very own son. He'd even thought of a name for him – Bjarki.

CHAPTER 1

Running as fast as he could on the log road that ran through the centre of Birka from the harbour to his house, Bjarki skidded to a halt as his mother appeared at the door.

'Mum, Dad says hurry up we need to set off for Log Island!'

'I'm just getting the rest of the picnic packed together,' said Signy checking her list. 'We don't want to forget any of your favourite things and spoil your birthday party now do we? I've got pickled herring, meatballs, rye bread, lingon jam, smultron and pear cider.'

'What about the Prinsesstårta? You can't forget that, it's my birthday cake.'

'Of course I haven't,' smiled Signy at her son as she ruffled his dark blond hair. With his colouring and piercing blue eyes, he was so like his father. 'I've made a special version for you. It looks like the cove you like north of the village, with the big grey rocks and birch trees, and there's even a model of your Dad's longship on it.'

'Oh cool. Can I see it?'

'When we get to Log Island,' said Signy, ushering Bjarki out of the house. 'I thought you said your Dad had sent you because we're running late.'

'Yes, come on,' said Bjarki, tugging his Mum's sleeve as they headed for the harbour, passing the wooden huts with turf roofs - some even had trees growing out of the roofs!

'Phew, I'm boiled,' said Bjarki, casting off his cloak and passing it to Signy.

'You're old enough to carry that yourself now you're ten,' she smiled, pushing it back to him. 'It's a perfect day for a picnic, isn't it.' Signy had been struck by the beautiful summers they had in Birka compared to Lofotr.

'Yes, I can't wait to get to Log Island.'

Soon they reached the harbour.

'Here comes the birthday boy,' announced Erik to everyone on board, as he saw Bjarki arrive at the quay with Signy. 'Here, pass me the picnic stuff,' he said to his wife, then helped her on board. Bjarki had already jumped down onto the ship and was chatting animatedly with his friends.

There was a slight breeze, the sky was clear perfect blue and the waters of Lake Mälar lapped gently against the side of the ship. Erik strode to the stern of the ship and took the tiller.

'OK chaps, heave ho - let's get this show on the road.' At that command the men of the village grabbed their oars, and pulled with all their might.

'Heeeeeave,' they shouted in unison as they rowed the boat out of the harbour.

It was a magnificent sight - the imposing Viking ship with a carved dragon's head at the front looked very grand as it skimmed through the sparkling blue water. Erik was still at the tiller when Bjarki came up to him, pushed forward by his group of friends.

'Dad, seeing as it's my birthday and it's windy, can we have the sail up pleeeeeeease?' asked Bjarki. He'd always liked the huge and impressive striped blue and yellow sail and had looked out for it coming back to the harbour when he was younger. He knew then his Dad was coming home.

'Let's just get out of the harbour, then we can set the sail,' replied Erik.

'That's brill. Can we help too?' said Bjarki.

Erik thought for a minute. 'I'm sure we can use some extra hands today. I'll give you a shout when we're putting it up.' Erik smiled as Bjarki and his friends pumped their fists and shouted 'Yessss!!'

'C'mon!' said Bjarki to his friends. 'I'll show

you my Dad's shield, he always keeps it on board. It'll be mine one day,' he said proudly. They ran down the deck. Bjarki rooted under one of the benches and dragged out a circular shield. It was royal blue with three yellow crowns on it, arranged in an inverted triangle with two at the top and one underneath. With an effort he held it upright and said, 'What d'you think?'

'Wow!'

'Cool!'

'Can I hold it?'

His friends were impressed.

'*My* Dad's shield's here too,' said one of the others, scrabbling under the next bench. 'Let's play warriors!' So whilst their fathers rowed, Bjarki and his friends pretended to fight off imaginary raiders. They also decided to 'attack' the on board 'enemy', frightening the life out of their mothers gathered in the bow talking about where best to set up the picnic!

The 'marauding' continued on board as the ship glided through the archipelago. The sound of the young voices echoing across the water mingled with the wind and the birdsong. Even the grey of the rocks shimmered silvery in the sunlight. There were thousands of islands: some large, some just rocks peeping above the water.

Bjarki was standing in the bow of the ship hanging onto the neck of the dragon. 'Look, there it is!' he shouted pointing ahead to Log Island. He ran down the other end. 'Dad we're nearly there. Where are we going to moor?'

'In the western bay I think will be best today,' replied Erik.

Log Island was a smallish island at the narrowest point, where the lake became the sea. It was a distinctive almost triangular island covered with trees. Erik always thought it would make an excellent strategic trading point and had talked to Bjarki about the idea.

Erik guided the longship into the bay. As soon as the ship was moored Bjarki and his friends jumped out continuing their game and all set to 'conquer' the new land.

The adults unloaded the ship. 'Don't go wandering too far now,' shouted Signy. 'We'll be having the picnic shortly.'

Too late - Bjarki had his cloth ears on, and ran with his friends over the grey rocks up the hill into the trees.

'C'mon! Let's play hide and seek.'

With all the trees and the big rocks there were loads of places to hide.

Bjarki was down near the southern tip of the island which was overshadowed by the cliffs on the island to the south, when he spotted what looked like a grotto. *What an excellent place to hide*, thought Bjarki, and went in.

It was very dark and damp inside the grotto. Bjarki could hear the water dripping off the rocks. He felt his way along the damp, slightly slimy rocky walls of the grotto. There was a glint of light twinkling deep in the cave. It was this mesmerising light that drew Bjarki ever deeper inside. He inched forward checking his footing so he didn't slip on the moisture-covered rock of the floor or any lichens and mosses that might be lurking there. Some had already trailed across his face making him jump.

The light that was drawing him was getting brighter and brighter as he got closer. At last he could see what it was - a small reddish-gold hammer no bigger than a teaspoon. Bjarki stretched his hand out towards it. Curiosity getting the better of him, he managed to reach out and grab hold of the little hammer. Suddenly he was thrown back and started spinning and spinning – he was in a vortex!

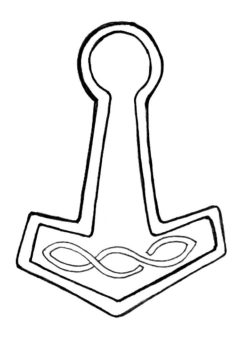

CHAPTER 2

Bjarki landed with a thud, face down in fine golden sand. He lay there a moment, a bit dazed. He lifted his head, shook it, and looked around him. In front was a vast sea. Behind him was a dark red rocky outcrop topped by birch trees and low bushes similar to Birka. There were huge mountains, off to the south-west in the distance, judging by the sun. Amazingly the little golden hammer was still in his hand. He put it in his pocket, stood up shakily and then brushed himself down.

Wow that was weird, thought Bjarki. *Where am I? It looks a bit like home but we don't have red rocks - we have grey ones and only a few of the nearby islands have sandy inlets. I think I'll head toward that hill and see what I can see from there.*

Bjarki started walking toward the hill. He was soon in the woods which reminded him of home.

I feel hungry, thought Bjarki. *I wonder if there are any smultron or lingon in these woods.* As he walked he alternated between looking where he was going and checking to see if there were any berries he could eat. There was no sign of life - maybe this place was uninhabited. It scared Bjarki to think he was all alone. After walking for about half an hour he came to a glade about half way to his destination. He spotted some leaves growing low to the ground that looked like wild strawberry plants.

'Oh yes – smultron!' Bjarki called out to no one and set about picking the berries and eating them. They were just as tasty at the ones on Birka and possibly a bit sweeter.

As he bent down to pick some more berries he heard a twig snap. Bjarki stood motionless. What was that? Without moving his head he looked down - he'd not trodden on anything. Was it an animal? Was it a person? His mind was racing, contemplating his options. Suddenly out of the corner of his eye he saw movement behind a tree. He started to move slowly toward it. The creature shot away and hid again - Bjarki inched forward carefully. There was a thick bush ahead. *I bet it's behind that*, thought Bjarki. He moved round one side as the other being moved away. It was like a game of tag. Eventually they bumped into each other back to back and both screamed and jumped out of their skins.

It was a girl about Bjarki's age. They looked at each other curiously.

'Who are you?' said the girl, in an accent that was similar to his Mum's. He could understand her though.

'My name is Bjarki. I am a Viking,' answered Bjarki. 'What's your name?'

'I am Alvi,' she replied looking him up and down. 'I am a Viking too.'

They were both dressed in skins and wool clothes.

'Where are we?' asked Bjarki

'This is Wirhale and I live over there in Greasby. My Dad has a farm there near the centre of the village,' Alvi replied, full of importance.

'Is this an island near Birka?' asked Bjarki

'I don't think so, but there is a headland of birch trees about an hour or so from here on foot called Birki that my Dad talks about. Is that where you mean?'

'I don't know, but we could check it out. Could you show me?'

Alvi hesitated. 'I really should be going home for my lunch. Mum sent me out to gather some berries. The wild strawberries like you were eating.'

'How did you know that?' asked Bjarki

'I was watching you for some time before you found me. Why don't you come back with me to my house for lunch? I guess you're still hungry the way you were scoffing those strawberries.'

Bjarki hesitated. He really wanted to find out if Birki was Birka and it was just the way Alvi pronounced it, but he was also starving out of his head.

'Will your Mum mind?'

As ever his stomach had won over his head.

'No, she likes it when I bring friends home. She's a great cook. She makes this really tasty stew called skaus. I bet you'll love it. We have the strawberries afterwards.'

Bjarki and Alvi set off for Alvi's house. It was up the hill a bit further. After about ten minutes they arrived.

'Mum, I'm back and I've brought a friend with me. That's ok isn't it?' shouted Alvi, as they came through the farmyard.

Alvi's Mum, who was called Liv, opened the door to the house. She was a pretty blonde woman of average height with an open friendly face.

'Hello there. Did you find the strawberries? And who is this?' asked Liv. She had not seen the other child before. He wasn't local.

'This is Bjarki. We met in the woods coming up from Meols. He's from Birki.' Alvi informed her Mum. 'He's really hungry. I spotted him eating the strawberries. He's a Viking like us but he's lost.'

'Hello Bjarki. Welcome. Do you like skaus?'

'I don't know. My Mum makes meatballs and I like those.'

'I'm sure you'll enjoy it. Sit down both of you and I'll dish up. Your Dad will be back any minute.' At that Liv shouted out of the back door. 'Rune, your lunch is ready and we have a guest so hurry up.'

Rune ambled into the house and sat at the head of the table.

'Hello young man. So you are our Alvi's friend.'

'Hello sir. Yes I am. My name is Bjarki.'

'Well Bjarki, sit down and let's eat lunch.'

Alvi was right, her Mum's skaus was delicious. Had his wooden bowl had a pattern on it Bjarki would have scraped it off.

'Would you like some more?' asked Liv.

'Yes please,' answered Bjarki eagerly.

So he had a second helping and still had room for strawberries.

'I like to see a lad with a good appetite,' remarked Rune. 'You'll need to be big and strong to row the longships when you're older.'

'Yes I know. I go out fishing and hunting with my Dad at home. Sometimes he lets me row our fishing boat for a while,' said Bjarki seriously.

Rune look suitably impressed and nodded sagely.

After lunch Alvi and Bjarki said they were going off back into the woods.

'You be careful now,' warned Liv. 'See you later.'

What they hadn't told her was that they were really going off to Birki!

CHAPTER 3

'So how do we get to this headland you mentioned?' muttered Bjarki, as they walked quickly out of the farmyard. They didn't want to arouse suspicion by running. Once round the corner Alvi pulled Bjarki down behind the low red sandstone wall.

'Look, we'll have to go carefully 'cos Dad'll be working in that field over there. If we go out through the woods we can loop back so he won't see us.'

'Ok, but are you sure you know how to get there?'

'Of course I do,' responded Alvi indignantly. 'I've been before with my parents. I am very good at remembering the way to places I've been to once before.'

'Girls are usually useless at directions,' replied Bjarki.

'Well I'm not, don't lump us all together. Do you want me to help you or not?'

Bjarki thought for a moment then shrugged. Alvi was his best bet – she knew the area and seemed alright – for a girl.

'Come on, hurry up before my Dad sees us.' Alvi tugged Bjarki's arm. She pulled him through a narrow gap between the hedge and the red sandstone wall.

'If we go up here we're hidden by the woods and then we come out at the top of the hill. It gets quite windy up there and all the trees are at strange angles but they all point the same way.'

'It's probably the wind that's done that,' said Bjarki. 'We have some like that on one of the islands in the archipelago on the eastern side of Log Island. That's what my Dad told me.'

They continued their travels for some time, then noticed there was a valley ahead of them and a bigger hill on the opposite side. 'Birki is over that hill and in about another half hour we'll be there,' advised Alvi.

They were now at the far edge of the wood looking across toward their destination. Suddenly they heard something behind them.

'I hope it's not Dad,' whispered Alvi, looking a bit alarmed. 'He'll go mad if he thinks we've wandered this far from the farm.'

It wasn't Rune but a couple of red squirrels running around across the ground and up the trees and along the branches. Leaves and nuts dropped down as the creatures went about their day collecting food for winter. *Aren't they cute?* thought Alvi.

'Have you seen squirrels before?' asked Alvi.

'Of course I have,' replied Bjarki. 'There's an island near home that has lots of squirrels on it. It's very beautiful and peaceful and has some flat plains in the centre that are good for farming. My uncle has a place there.'

They continued their trip without much more by way of surprises until they reached quite a wide river in a steep-sided valley.

'We need to walk along by the river now to get to Birki,' Alvi informed Bjarki.

'This doesn't look very familiar to me,' replied Bjarki. 'I'm starting to wonder what's happening today.'

At that he felt a vibrating in his pocket. He looked up - Alvi had started walking again.

'Hang on,' called Bjarki. He reached into his pocket and brought out the little golden hammer.

'What's that?' asked Alvi, thinking how pretty it was and how she would like to have one too.

At that moment the hammer started glowing and vibrating again.

Oh heck thought Bjarki, *it's going to start doing something. How am I going to explain this to Alvi?* Bjarki was about to make an excuse, when Mjolnir started its rhyme.

'Did you say something?' asked Alvi, suspiciously.

'No, no it wasn't m....' Bjarki stopped himself.

'But I heard a voice like you were making fun of my accent.'

'No I wasn't, I mean didn't.'

'You did. I'm trying to help you and now you're making fun of me. I thought we were friends.'

'We are. It wasn't me. Can I tell you a secret?'

'Ok, what is it?' queried Alvi.

'I found this little hammer when I was playing hide and seek with my friends, and it does strange things like glows and vibrates........and talks.....in rhyme.'

'Yep, right and I'm a troll,' replied Alvi. 'Are you a crazy boy?'

'No, I'm telling you the truth. Look.' Bjarki opened his hand and showed her the hammer.

Alvi looked at it. Apart from being very shiny it didn't look that special or very different from some of her Mum's jewellery.

'It just looks like something from a necklace,' said Alvi.

The hammer just lay in Bjarki's hand doing nothing. *Typical!* thought Bjarki, *Why has it decided to shut up now?* Bjarki looked hard at the hammer willing it to speak again but - nothing.

'Honest, I heard it, it spoke!"

'So what did it say?' asked Alvi with a hint of sarcasm in her voice.

Bjarki repeated the rhyme as he'd heard it.

'At the sandbank of crane
Will you search in vain?'

'It makes no sense to me,' said Bjarki, but Alvi was looking very pensive. Sandbank of cranes she thought. Suddenly – **ping!** - it struck her.

'Bjarki, the sandbank of cranes is at the end of this river on the other side! There's a bridge about five minutes from here. Come on, let's see what it is!'

They raced toward the bridge – they didn't know it yet, but their adventure had begun!

32

CHAPTER 4

When they reached the bridge they stopped half way across to watch the water flowing rapidly underneath. Looking north toward the estuary Bjarki spotted a crane by the side of the water.

'Look, there's one.'

He pointed it out to Alvi. When she looked up she saw what looked more like a troll, not a crane.

'Shhhh,' said Alvi, quietly. 'It looks like there are trolls here abouts.'

Alvi pointed. Bjarki looked and, sure enough, there was a troll staring back at him.

'What do we do now?' whispered Bjarki. 'Are they friendly, these trolls?'

'I don't know, there are some very playful trolls around here all with different colour hair. It's the rainbow haired trolls that are completely crazy but very friendly – and they can transform into different things. There's a set of rainbow troll twins in my class at school. They're brother and sister but identical to look at. It's a troll thing.' said Alvi knowledgably.

The pair edged steadily forward. The trolls kept pinging up all over the place randomly, in different forms or as themselves, and making Alvi and Bjarki jump. It seemed like a really good game to the trolls. All of a sudden the twins from Alvi's class appeared on the track directly in front of them.

'Hi Alvi,' they chorused. They always spoke together, usually saying the same thing but occasionally they said different things at once – very confusing.

'How did you like our new disguises?'

'Hi Inge and Inga,' replied Alvi. 'You mean it was you two all along? What are you doing down here?'

'Yep it was, cool disguises don't you think? Did you like the giant red toadstool with the domherre on the top? We've just perfected that,' they said proudly.

'I'm the toadstool,' said Inge and 'I'm the bird,' said Inga at the same time. It was so confusing when they spoke at once but said different things.

'We're visiting our aunty. She lives in that hole over there.' The twins pointed through the trees.

Bjarki couldn't make the hole out among the undergrowth but didn't like to say.

'What are you doing down here Alvi? And

who's this? Your new boyfriend?' questioned the twins. 'Alvi's got a boyfriend, Alvi's got a boyfriend, na na nan na naa,' the trolls sang tunelessly as they danced around the pair.

'No I haven't, this is my friend Bjarki, he's lost and I'm helping him try and get back home.'

'Hee hee hee, he's lost,' chanted the twins continuing their crazy dance.

Bjarki was embarrassed and not best pleased at being introduced as 'lost'.

'Yes, well we're heading toward Birka and the sandbank so not far now,' commented Bjarki, seeking to improve his status from 'lost'.

'We're going that way too. Want to see if we can catch some fish. We'll come with you,' replied Inge and Inga.

Oh great thought Bjarki, *these two are crazy - but I suppose they seem friendly enough.*

The four of them set off, the twins running, jumping, gamboling and leap-frogging their way to the sandbank, chattering the whole time. About what, Bjarki couldn't hear. He was intrigued at how they changed form, then back to themselves, or was it each other? It was hard to tell.

'Come on you two hurry up,' shouted the twins. Trolls move much faster than humans so Bjarki and Alvi were running as fast as they could but getting out of breath trying to keep up.

'Slow down and keep the noise down,' Alvi puffed between catching her breath. 'We don't want the monks to hear us.'

There was a church down by the river.

'Wait 'til we get round that bend, there's loads by the estuary but we don't want them to see us.'

'Who, the monks?' asked the twins

'No, I meant the cranes,' replied Alvi

'What are monks?' asked Bjarki, still on the earlier bit of the conversation. Trolls easily cause confusion.

'Monks are very religious men who all live together in a house next to the church.'

'You mean we're going to Asgard?' queried Bjarki. 'Wow, it would be so cool to meet Thor in person or to see Frigg. She's supposed to be the ultimate beauty, so I've heard my Dad and Uncle say.'

'What are you talking about? Who are these people Thor and Frigg?'

'They're the gods we worship.'

'Oh, I assumed you were Christian like me.'

'No, I guess not. Is that a problem?'

'No, actually my Gran used to talk about Odin and Frey. Are they some of your gods too?

She thinks my parents are heathens choosing Christianity over the traditional Norse gods.'

'Yes of course, Odin is our chief god. There's a whole load of them live in Asgard.'

'Is Asgard near where you live?' asked Alvi.

'I don't know, I've not been there.'

They continued walking in silence, the trolls tiptoeing in an exaggerated manner. The path by the river was well used and easy to follow. They soon reached the estuary and the sandbank. The sand was gold-coloured and there were lumps of dark red rock of different sizes scattered across the shore as well as some very pretty flowers and quite a few jelly fish. The cranes stood randomly around the sandbank at first, not taking any notice of the newly arrived visitors.

'What are we looking for?' asked Alvi.

'Yes, what are we looking for?' echoed Inga and Inge.

'I'm not sure,' replied Bjarki

'Why are you here then?' asked the twins.

'We're going to find some fish.'

The trolls ran to the shoreline and transformed into a boat to go fishing, then changed themselves into sharks once in the water.

'This is where the hammer told me to come to,' said Bjarki replying to Alvi's question and glad that Inge and Inga had found something else to do.

Alvi looked unsure. 'Shouldn't we just forget about the hammer? I thought you were trying to get home. Look, that's Birki over there so you're home and I can head back to Greasby. I should just make it in time for tea.'

Bjarki clenched his fists. 'You just don't get it do you Alvi. That's not Birka. It's not my home town. I'm lost in a place I've never been before and you and your Mum and Dad are the only people I know. You can't just leave me here. I don't know why I'm here or what I'm trying to find. You've got to help me.'

'No I don't,' retorted Alvi. 'I'm going home. See you bye, been nice knowing you. The trolls will help you - they'll be back soon.'

Alvi started to move off. Bjarki grabbed her sleeve.

'No wait - please stay and help me. Don't get me wrong, I like Inge and Inga but they're as mad as a box of frogs. Look, I'll let you look after the little hammer.'

Alvi still wasn't sure, but she *did* like the little gold hammer. Bjarki took it out of his pocket to give to her.

'Here you are, you carry it for a while.'

Bjarki held the hammer out to Alvi. As she went to take it it started to glow again and seemed to be glued to Bjarki's hand.

'Hey, stop messing about, just give me the hammer,' insisted Alvi.

'I can't, it won't move from my hand. It's stuck!'

'Don't be soft. You just don't want to give it to me, do you?'

'Yes I do.'

At that the hammer started vibrating again.

'What are you doing now?' challenged Alvi.

'Nothing,' replied Bjarki, looking puzzled.

At that the hammer started its rhyme again:

At the sandbank of crane
You will search in vain
Go to the hazel well
There you'll hear a bell.'

Alvi looked stunned.

'How did you do that?' she demanded.

'It wasn't me, it was the hammer.'

'Yes, well looks like you got the rhyme wrong. It said *you will* search in vain not *will you* search in vain. Whatever it is you are looking for it isn't here. We should be the other side of the peninsula.

That's where the hazel well is, at least the only one I know of around these parts.'

'Wait a minute, you said peninsula. You mean this isn't an island we're on?'

'Correct, clever clogs. We're attached to the mainland down near Chester but we don't go there 'cos they're not Vikings. In fact it's only really the northern end of the peninsula that's inhabited by Vikings - the rest are Saxons, or Celts or something. There was a big battle at Bromborough and we won so we got to stay here. My Grandad remembers living many miles away in a land where the sun never sets in summer and never rises in winter. How weird is that? Mind you he tells me that on a winter night he used to watch the multicoloured lights dancing around in the sky which sounds truly amazing. It would be brilliant to see that. He also said it was quite cold compared to here.'

'That sounds a bit like the place my Mum's from. When she met Dad she moved to live in his house, which was a good few months by boat from her home in Lofotr. It's warmer here than at home by me just now. So, what about that land over there?' questioned Bjarki, pointing to the land visible across the river about a mile away, with an inlet that looked like a natural pool or harbour.

'I don't know. I think Dad and some of the other men have been there once but there wasn't anything much of interest there so they've not been back since. In any case what do you want to do about getting to the hazel well? We won't get there and back to my house today if we're on foot. It's too far.'

'Look in that field up there.'

Bjarki pointed up the hill. There was a horse. 'We could 'borrow' that horse, that'd be quicker. I can ride and if you know the way you can direct me.'

'Yes and what about me - will I be running behind?' asked Alvi.

'No we can both get on it.'

They made their way up the short hill and collected some fresh tasty grass on the way to tempt the horse over with. After a short while the horse, which seemed quite tame, came and ate the proffered grass. As Alvi distracted it Bjarki jumped on its back. It didn't seem to mind. Then Bjarki helped Alvi up behind him.

'Hold on tight,' he called as they set off. 'Which way am I going?'

'Back the way we came until you get to the second hill top, then follow the ridge south.' As the path opened out into the heathland Bjarki urged the horse on to a gallop, and they sped through the countryside.

CHAPTER 5

'Way Hay,' shouted Bjarki. 'This is great. I love riding. This horse is as fast as the trolls.'

'It *is* us!' chorused the twins, transforming back and dumping their riders in a heap in the process.

'I didn't see you leave the river,' replied Alvi.

'No? That's 'cos we emerged as frogs and once we'd hopped by you we changed to rabbits, shot up the hill to the field and became Dobbin, the horse.'

'I did wonder how we'd managed to tame the horse so easily,' added Bjarki.

'Can you go into horse mode again please and get us to the hazel well quickly?' Alvi asked.

'Ok. Come on hop up,' replied the twins, now Dobbin.

Galloping along the ridge Bjarki noticed an impressive avenue of tall stones leading to a flat topped mound.

'Is that Tingvall?' asked Bjarki.

'Yes, we are at Thingwall. How did you know that if you've never been here before?' Alvi was puzzled.

'It's very like the one at Anundshög at home. Is there a maze as well?'

'No,' replied Alvi shyly, 'but there is one near Irby. Mum tells me about when she lived in the land of the midnight sun how she stood in the middle of the maze and waited for Dad to find his way through to her. It was very romantic.'

'Yuk, how soppy is that?' retorted Bjarki.

'Sooooo soppy, soppy, soppy,' chanted the trolls, still in their disguise as Dobbin.

Soon they reached the hazel well. It was in a little gorge-like valley that led down to the waterside. A stream trickled down the valley which was overhung with trees. That must be hazel, thought Bjarki.

'Whoaaa.' Bjarki reined Dobbin to stop. Again the twins stopped, by just becoming themselves and dumping Bjarki and Alvi on the ground.

'I wish you'd give us some warning,' said Bjarki, brushing the soil and leaves off himself.

'But you said to stop so we did,' the trolls pointed out.

'They have a point,' said Alvi.

'We're going to look for berries. Just call if you need us.' Chatting conspiratorially the twins ran and skipped away down the little gorge.

'So what did the rhyme say?' asked Alvi

'I don't know, something about a bell,' said Bjarki, 'Do you think it's down the well or something? Tell you what, I'll climb into the bucket and you wind it down and I'll see what I can find.'

'How will you see what's down there?'

'Good point. Maybe we can find some birch bark – I've got a flint so maybe we can make a fire and then a torch?'

'In any case, I'm lighter than you,' remarked Alvi. 'Maybe it'd be better if I went in the bucket and you wound the handle.'

Bjarki had to admit there was some sense in that as he was stronger so could wind the bucket up and down more easily. Bjarki pulled the bucket to the side of the well and helped Alvi climb in. He lit the birch bark and handed it to her, then started to slowly wind the bucket and Alvi down into the well.

'What can you see?' called Bjarki.

'Not a lot. It's damp and cold and a bit smelly down here. Yuk, what was that?' The bucket was swinging a bit and Alvi caught the side of the well.

Moss, lichen and ferns can be quite scary in the semi-dark when unexpected.

The wind had been blowing from the north east until then and now it turned to the south west. As that happened, Bjarki heard the sound of a distant bell.

'I can hear a bell ringing,' announced Bjarki. 'Can you?'

'No, I can't see or hear anything down here and the bark has gone out.'

The bell tolled again.

'I don't think the bell is down there. I think it's the one I can hear ringing,' said Bjarki.

'Can you wind the bucket back up then?' called Alvi.

With a lot of effort Bjarki returned Alvi and the bucket to the daylight and helped her out. She was looking a bit grubby and dishevelled but Bjarki didn't really notice.

'Any ideas where that bell is?' asked Bjarki. 'The hammer said we'd hear a bell didn't it?'

'It did,' said Alvi.

'Well that must be the bell.'

'Let's head towards it.'

'You'd better call Inge and Inga.'

'They're probably down at the beach. It's only just down there.'

They headed off down the valley as the trolls had done. When they reached the beach there was no sign of the trolls or Dobbin, only two seals.

'I bet that's them,' said Bjarki pointing at the seals.

'I don't think so, they've not done that disguise before,' replied Alvi.

At that Bjarki noticed one of the seals was wearing braces.

'It's them. Look that one has braces on.'

'Inge, Inga, any chance of another ride on Dobbin please?' asked Alvi.

'We're enjoying sun bathing,' replied the twins, still in their seal forms.

'But we need to get to West Church Village. Can I tempt you to a nice gallop along the beach? C'mon, it's not far and you can sunbathe there too.'

The seals chatted and then – ping! - they were trolls again, and then Dobbin.

Bjarki ran to mount the horse. 'Come on Alvi.'

He helped her up onto the horse and set off in the direction of the sound.

'Do you know where we're going?' asked Alvi.

'No, but what's in this direction that's got a bell?'

'Oh, I know, there's a new church just up the coast. We need to follow the river. The village has grown since the church was built and it's not far from Greasby, so we could be back home before dark. The church is named after St Bridget.'

'Let's go!'

CHAPTER 6

They set off at a gallop along the beach.

The hammer suddenly woke up again and spouted:

'From the church in the west
Where you will be a guest
There by the track
Lies the hogback.'

'Sounds like we're headed in the right direction,' said Bjarki. 'But I don't see any pigs. Come on Dobbin.' He encouraged the 'horse' to move by jabbing it in the ribs with his heels.

They cantered along the beach as it was the fastest and most direct route from the well to the church. The sun was still high in the sky and it lit up the mountains across the river.

'Those are big hills,' remarked Bjarki.

'Yes, I think Mum and Dad tried to settle over there before they moved here. The locals weren't too friendly and the ground was poor for farming so Dad says we are far better off here on Wirhale,' said Alvi.

The red sandstone cliffs rose directly up from the beach quite steeply with few opportunities to leave the shore. But it was great fun riding unhindered along the sand and occasionally through the water as the waves hit the beach.

'It's so beautiful and peaceful here,' remarked Bjarki. 'It reminds me of Birka and especially of Log Island. That's my fave place. In fact that's where today started out. It's my birthday and we were having a special picnic on Log Island to celebrate. I'm ten today.'

'Are you? Happy Birthday! I'm ten in a few months too,' said Alvi.

The cliffs were starting to get a bit smaller and there was a more gentle slope ahead.

'I think we can go up there,' said Alvi, pointing, 'and it'll take us to the church.'

Bjarki slowed the horse to a stop to look in the direction Alvi indicated.

'Giddy up Dobbin,' they both exclaimed simultaneously and the horse trotted up the slope.

'See those trees,' Alvi pointed again. 'The church is near those.'

Bjarki steered the horse to the left and slowed to a walk. There were a lot of birch trees and heather and various well trodden paths as they neared the church and the village. Then Bjarki spotted a narrow track running parallel with the bottom of the sandstone outcrop and headed along it. It opened out into a flatter area with trees around and there stood the church with its separate bell tower. They took the outer track round the church and that's when they espied the hogback.

'Bjarki, look that must be it!' exclaimed Alvi. 'The hammer said there by the track you'll find a hogback. It's a stone one not a real pig like you thought.'

Bjarki tried to hide his embarrassment. He decided just to rein in Dobbin this time rather than asking the twins to stop, so he and Alvi just jumped down from its back. Once they were on the ground and the twins realised they were 'riderless' they became themselves again.

'We're going back to the beach to sunbathe. Let us know if you want us for anything.' Off they went in their usual ramshackle way of running, leap-frogging, transforming, one after the other.

Bjarki turned his attention back to the hogback.

'That is so cool. It looks a bit like the runestones we have at home. It's even got writing on it. The ones at home usually tell stories of great bravery or loss in battle. They cost a lot to have made. I know there is one for my Great Grandfather somewhere on the southern shore of Lake Mälar. Dad said when I am older he'll take me there to see it. He was a very brave and important warrior.'

At that the hammer started its performance again – glowing and vibrating.

'What's it going to tell us now?' asked Alvi

'Shhh, listen,' said Bjarki putting a finger to his lips.

The hammer then intoned:

'Touch it and see
Just where you'll then be.'

'What do you think?' asked Bjarki. 'Should we touch it?'

'Well, we've come this far we might as well,' encouraged Alvi.

'Look, give me your hand just in case something odd happens,' said Bjarki and took Alvi's hand. With his free hand he touched the hogback.

Oh no! thought Bjarki, not twice in one day! The flying sensation, spinning rapidly through the air like in a vortex – it was happening again!

And this time there were two of them in the vortex!

CHAPTER 7

Splat!

Bjarki and Alvi landed unceremoniously in a large clump of heather which at least broke their fall. Bjarki had landed first and Alvi got the even softer landing on him.

'Get off me,' said an irritated Bjarki. Alvi moved.

'There's no need to be like that. It wasn't my fault we landed in a heap on the heather. I'm just glad it was the heather and not one of those big boulders or that gorse bush over there.'

'Yep, those boulders look like something Thor would throw if he was really angry,' commented Bjarki.

'Oh you and your pagan gods,' responded Alvi in an aloof tone. Then as they both stood up she went quiet and stared at Bjarki and he at her.

Bjarki stood there looking down at the strange

garments he was wearing. They were comfortable and softer than the wool and skins he was used to. His trousers were dark blue, and he also was wearing a blue shirt with three yellow crowns on it, coincidentally arranged in the same format as on the shield his Dad had on his longship, and white shoes with harder soles than his normal shoes. Instead of his metal helmet he had a soft foamy one with horns. It was cross patched blue and yellow and the horns were yellow. Very tasteful!

Alvi was dressed the same but her top was red with white and blue cross trimmings on the shoulders, and instead of the three crowns there was a lion rampant on her top. Her helmet was red with one blue and one white horn.

'Wow, these are cool clothes,' commented Alvi.

As they looked around they realised that the area had also changed. Yes, they were still on the big red stones on the hill, but they could see strange buildings made of stone with hard roofs and different coloured metal boxes on wheels moving of their own accord (or so it seemed) along a wide grey ribbon at the foot of the hill.

One of the metal boxes stopped just as Alvi was watching it. A door opened and a person got out.

'Look there Bjarki, those boxes have people in them.'

'Wicked! I wish we could try one. C'mon Alvi, let's head down to that grey track.'

They ran and jumped over the red rocks and through between the heather and the gorse bushes.

Bjarki stopped suddenly.

'Alvi look! There's a whole load of sleeping metal boxes over there. Shall we see if we can wake one up?'

They approached the boxes carefully. They were all different sizes and some were quite big close up.

Suddenly there was a roar behind them. They jumped in surprise. A metal box was approaching, moving into a space near them. They hid behind one of the others and watched as the occupants alighted.

'C'mon quickly,' whispered Bjarki urgently. 'Let's get in the back while they're not looking and hide there.'

They climbed in the back. Then all the doors were shut and they heard a 'klunk'.

'What was that noise?' asked Alvi

'I don't know,' replied Bjarki. He moved toward the big door at the back that he'd seen open upwards before. 'It's stuck. I can't open it.'

'We're trapped. Great idea Bjarki! So now what?'

'We could climb into the front if it wasn't for this grill. Maybe we can loosen it?'

'Or we could wait 'til they get back and unklunk it.'

Bjarki tried to budge the grill but it wasn't moving. He sat back exasperated and frustrated.

'I guess we'll have to wait,' he begrudgingly acknowledged.

After what seemed like ages they heard a 'klunk' again - the people must be coming back!

'Let's get out,' whispered Alvi. 'Quick!'

'No, we wanted to ride in one of these. Let's stay, they've not spotted us yet!'

With that they both hunkered down, pulled a nearby rug over them and waited for the start of their mystery tour.

CHAPTER 8

The metal box owners climbed in the front. The box roared into life and shot backwards before being swung round and moved slowly forwards. There was a light clicking noise which stopped once they had turned left. Off they went faster and faster. It was a very weird but exciting feeling, better even than galloping along the beach on the horse.

'This is fun,' whispered Alvi.
'Too right. It's better than the longships and it goes faster than horses on land. Amazing!'

After about twenty minutes the machine stopped briefly and part of it must have opened because the sound changed, and then they heard the sound of coins being dropped into a box.
The next thing they knew they were going down a gentle slope as though deep underground. Peeping out from under the rug they could see

bright lights speeding by overhead as they lay in the back of the metal box. Alvi felt a bit scared but didn't want Bjarki to know.

After another quarter of an hour, having exited the tunnel they stopped. As the box was manoeuvred into a space, they saw three huge buildings nearby.

'Look at those,' whispered Alvi.

'Hey, I like those birds on the top of that end one. I wonder what type they are? Eagles maybe?'

'Shall we take a look?'

At that, the doors unklunked.

'Quick, this is our chance to get out.'

Bjarki and Alvi slipped out of the back of the metal box unnoticed and started toward the tallest of the three buildings – the one with the birds on top.

'How are we going to get up there?' asked Alvi.

'No idea but we could try that strange looking door over there.'

Bjarki pointed to what looked like a door going round and round. People were going into it and some were being spat out again.

'It looks like people go in that way and get catapulted into the building. Let's try it.'

They walked up the steps to the strange-looking door and watched as people took turns entering the door from both sides and exiting the opposite side. Then one man decided to go all the way round and not come out after all.

'Come on let's try it,' said Bjarki.

They stood close together waiting for the right time to enter the twirling door, then stepped in. They ended up going round one and a half times before finding themselves in the building. It was most impressive and the biggest building they could ever imagine. There were lots of people going in and out and about their business so that no one really paid any heed to them in their jeans and football tops.

Bjarki noticed a group of people waiting outside some doors, looking up at coloured shapes lighting up one at a time. When the green curled arrow shape lit up, the doors opened and people got out of yet another type of metal box. The small group waiting then got into the box. Alvi and Bjarki joined them. There were buttons on the side and various people pushed different ones. The metal box's doors closed and then started moving upwards.

'My tummy feels funny,' said Alvi, 'like I've just left it behind.'

'Mine too,' replied Bjarki, looking a little green.

At that the doors opened and some people got out. More got in and one of them pressed the top button.

Bjarki whispered to Alvi, 'Let's get out when he does. That must be the top by the birds.'

They did as Bjarki suggested but when they got out they found there were some steps to climb to get onto the roof.

'Come on, hurry.' Bjarki waved Alvi in the direction of the steps.

Soon they were on the roof and saw the birds and just how big they really were. But they weren't real after all - they weren't moving.

From where they were they could see the sun starting to set across the water. It was stunning. There were a few other people on the roof, and one remarked, 'Look at all those cranes on the bank over there. You can even see the old church where the monks used to be and rowed the ferry over the river.'

'Yes that'll be Tranmere and Monks Ferry in Birkenhead,' replied the other adult.

Bjarki had a feeling of déjà vu as if he should recognise the place across the river but he couldn't quite bring it to mind. Alvi and Bjarki stared off into the distance, both lost in thought.

Before too long they realised they were the only people left on the roof, and it was already dusk. Suddenly they heard a hissing noise.

'Psst! Psst! Ey you down der! You two kidz in de funny cozzies.'

Bjarki and Alvi looked at each other.

'Did you hear someone speak?' asked Alvi.

'Ey dozy, it woz me. I'm Paul and thah's me missiz Livvy down de other end. You aw'right?'

Bjarki realised it was the big bird that was talking to them in that strange way.

'Yes we're fine,' answered Bjarki, not knowing what else to say to a metal bird that by rights shouldn't be talking at all.

'No yer not,' laughed Paul, 'yer stuck up 'ere on dis roof wiv us for de night.'

At that Bjarki felt a vibration in his pocket again. It was the little gold hammer still with him. He took it out of his pocket.

'Wot you got dere den?' asked the bird.

'N – n - nothing,' stammered Bjarki.

'Don't talk daft, I can see yer got summat. Warrisit?'

Warily Bjarki showed it to Paul.

'Ey Livvy, look at dis. De kid's gorra gold hammer like de one we saw in de museum when de teeam was in Sweeden. You know when we thrashed dat udder team wid de funny spelt name.'

'You mean Deyourgarden or however de sed it?' said Livvy.

'Yeh, dat's it. So are yer from dere? Y' know, Sweeden.'

'No,' said Alvi indignantly, 'I'm from Wirhale.'

'Oh get you, a posh Scouser eh from over de water, y'know, de Wirral.'

'I'm from Birka, I'm a Viking,' announced Bjarki.

'Yeh I can see from yer titfer yer from Scandinavia. When are yer goin' bach?'

'I don't know,' said Bjarki, suddenly feeling homesick.

'Ey! I've gorra great idea! Me and our Livvy can give yer a lift if yer quick.'

'What do you mean?' asked Alvi

'Well we can fly y' der dead quick, and cheaper dan dese budget airlines, us Liver Birds y' know. C'mon, hop up. You lad, gerron me bach and yer geerl can go wiv de missiz.'

'Ok, if you're sure you won't be missed,' said Bjarki.

'Lucky for us de lights have shorted and dey've not fixed 'em yet, so no one'll see we're missin' for a few hours.'

With that the four of them set off flying into the night. Bjarki and Alvi held onto the birds for dear life – they soon found out that Liver Birds fly very quickly and at high speed.

'This is amazing,' shouted Alvi to Bjarki across the sky.
'How do you know where to go?' Bjarki asked Paul.
'Dat's eazy. Like I sed, we flew over to dere for de footie de other week. We thrashed your lot. I saw de free crowns like on yer shert on de top of a brown buildin' in de centre of de city. We'll drop you der, it must be near your place.'

After what seemed like only the blink of an eye the birds glided down on the air streams and towards the bright lights sparkling off the water of the lake.

'Der's de brown buildin' I saw before. See, it's got dem der gold crowns on the top, told yer,' said Paul.

Bjarki looked down. Just south of the brown building he could make out a heavily built-up triangular island and also some cliffs on the island just south of that. Again Bjarki felt it looked familiar but couldn't quite place why.

He was still contemplating this when Paul and Livvy landed on the grass just below the tower at the corner of the brown building with the crowns on top and just by the lake.

'Y'd better geroff quick 'cos we can't be seen 'ere. We should be in Liverpool not Stockholm.'

'Did you say 'Stockholm'?' queried Bjarki. 'That means Log Island! Oh thanks so much Paul for bringing me home!'

'No probs lad.'

Bjarki didn't like to mention the fact it looked very different, but somehow it held an air of familiarity. At least he was home, but how was he going to explain Alvi to his Mum and Dad?

The Liver Birds flew off.

'Thanks for the lift,' called the two friends. 'See you again soon!'

'Ta ra kidz,' called Livvy and Paul, as with two flaps of their mighty wings they disappeared into the night.

CHAPTER 9

'So what now,' asked Alvi. 'Where are we?'

'Well it seems we're back almost to where I found the little hammer in the grotto,' said Bjarki, frowning. 'You see that island over there? It looks the same shape as the one I call Log Island and those cliffs look similar, but everything else is totally different. I think we must be in the future. I'm not sure how we're going to get back to Viking times but at least if we are on Log Island maybe there'll be some way of finding a way back.'

'That's fine for you but what about me?' asked Alvi. 'I'm miles from home and my Mum will be getting worried. I should have been back hours ago. In any case, how are we going to get over to your Log Island?'

'I think we can walk round there. It looks like there are paths of smooth flat stone to walk on between the lake and those huge buildings. Let's go.'

Bjarki started walking toward the exit through the arches of the building facing the lake and into the courtyard aiming for the big wooden doors on the far side.

He turned right and headed round following the northern lakeside shore. There were bridges now instead of the boats to get between the islands, and his Dad had been right to think it would make a really good place for a trading centre. It was a very busy but very open relaxing-looking settlement, much bigger than any Bjarki had ever seen. It was a truly beautiful city, like a shiny jewel in the dark blue waters of the lake.

They crossed to the island with the church with the ornate metal steeple and then on to the triangular one with all its narrow winding streets. They walked to the top of the hill into the Big Square with its tall thin prettily-painted buildings in red, yellow, green and brown.

'Which way shall we go, d'you think?' Alvi asked.

'Down here,' suggested Bjarki.

This was a narrow street with mainly yellow ochre-painted tall thin terraced buildings. Eventually they arrived at a very impressive looking statue of a man on a horse fighting with a dragon. Below the mound on which the statue stood, Bjarki noticed there was a door in the rock which was slightly ajar.

'Let's hide in here and decide what to do,' said Bjarki.

They went through the door.......into a grotto.

It had been a long day and the two of them sat down to decide what they could do to get home to their own time and place. They soon dozed off.

The next thing Bjarki knew was that he could hear voices calling his name. Then he thought he heard his Mum singing in that unmistakeably rich beautiful voice that echoed through you to the core. He shook himself to wake up.

'Mum, Dad I'm here. Mum, Dad where are you?'

Then his father's face appeared through a narrow gap at the entrance to the cave.

'Bjarki we've been looking for you for ages! Where have you been? Come out of there.'

Erik moved a stone that had partially blocked the entrance.

Bjarki shook his head and blinked. 'I was playing hide and seek and hid in the cave. I must have fallen asleep. I had this really weird dream... I'll tell you all about it. Where's......'

Bjarki didn't finish the sentence. His Mum, Signy, had appeared at the opening and he rushed to her. Signy enveloped him in her arms and said, 'Well you gave us quite a fright! We've been looking for you for nearly half an hour.' Bjarki frowned but didn't say anything. His mother finally let him go and said, 'Shall we start the party now? There's all that food to be eaten! And guess what! My sister and her family arrived today.'

Just then a girl appeared from behind Signy.

'Bjarki, this is your cousin.' Signy looked at her son, who was staring open-mouthed. 'Aren't you going to say hello to her Bjarki? Her name's…'

'Alvi!'

Alvi smiled knowingly and winked…

THE END

AFTERWORD
FROM THE AUTHOR

In case you were wondering...the 'j' in Bjarki and Mjolnir is pronounced like the 'y' in 'you'!

And the Norwegian Vikings (or Bay dwellers) *did* inhabit the northern part of the Wirral peninsula some time around 900AD. They originally settled in Eire near Dublin before heading across the Irish Sea and trying unsuccessfully to live in Wales. It is chronicled in Ingimund's Saga that they were given lands 'north of Chester'. The place names which still exist to this day on the Wirral support this, as do finds of Viking ships in Meols and genetic testing of people from the Wirral, whose DNA matches very closely to modern day Norwegians.

The places on the Wirral (Wirhale in Viking times) referred to in the story include:

Meols (pronounced Mells), meaning the sandbanks.

Greasby, meaning stronghold in the woods.

Birkenhead is Birki, meaning headland of birch trees.

Monk's Ferry (the church is still there).

Tranmere, meaning sandbank of cranes (it's just the metal rather than the feathered variety these days!).

Thingwall (Tingvall in Scandinavia), meaning field where the assembly or parliament meet.

Heswall (pronounced Hezwool), meaning Hazel well.

West Kirby, meaning West Church Village (St Bridget's Church and the hogback are still there).

Thurstaston, meaning Thor's stones (as I was always told by my Dad), or more probably Thorsteins Farm (you can see the red boulders which some believe are Mjolnir still!).

Bromborough, meaning border settlement on the border of the Viking lands with other peoples to the south and site of a key battle in English history in 937AD.

Liverpool as such did not exist in Viking times - it was just an inlet and harbour. Today you can go into the Liver Buildings on the Pier Head and even arrange a visit to the roof to get a closer look at the Liver Birds.

In the very north of Norway on the Lofotens, you can still visit Lofotr, near Leknes. A huge Viking longhouse has been reconstructed next to the foundations of the real one. It was the home of a very important Viking king or earl. You can see how the Vikings lived, the animals they kept and also take a trip on a Viking longship.

Also, as I discovered while on holiday in Norway, you can buy tins of lapskaus, or as it is called in English lob scouse, and it tastes exactly the same as the dish my Nana used to make for me and which is still served today on Merseyside. It is this Viking foodstuff which gave its name to the slang name for people from Liverpool – Scousers. My Nana's recipe is set out at the end of this section, in case you want to try it.

In Sweden the island of Bjorkö (or Birch Island in English) was the location of the original Swedish Viking settlement of Birka. You can visit Birka in the summer. It is about an hour west of Stockholm by boat. You can also see a reconstruction of life in Birka in Viking times at Historiska Museet (the Historical Museum) in Stockholm.

Today Stockholm is Sweden's capital city and spreads across 14 main islands at the point where Lake Mälar (pronounced Merlar) meets the Baltic Sea. Stockholm itself means Log Island in English and Gamla Stan (the Old Town) is roughly triangular in shape, overshadowed by the cliffs of Södermalm (South Island) (pronounced Sirdermalm) to the south. Another of Stockholm's main islands today is called Djurgården (the Royal Deer Park) or as the chatty Liver Birds called it - Deyourgarden. The brown building described with the three crowns on top is Stockholm City Hall (Stadshuset). You can take a tour of the building and also climb up the tower. The church with the metal steeple is Riddarholm Church (Riddarholmkyrka), which is where most of Sweden's kings and queens are buried. The Big Square mentioned is Stortorget (pronounced 'Stortoryet' and which means the big square) on Gamla Stan.

Anundshög is a small village east of Västerås (pronounced Vesteros) on the northern shores of Lake Mälar, not too far by boat from Birka. It has some of the most important Viking finds in Sweden including burial mounds, standing stones laid out in the shape of ships, a grand avenue of standing stones and a maze. They think it was a very important Viking queen who was buried here as they have found a lot of women's possessions.

You can try all Bjarki's favourite foods even today with some supermarkets stocking Swedish meatballs (köttbullar, pronounced shertbuller), rye bread (a dark brown heavy square sliced bread), Prinsesstårta (a sponge, jam and cream cake normally covered in green marzipan, sometimes sold as Princess Tart or Festival cake in the UK) and pickled herring (sill). Smultron (wild strawberries) can be found on country walks if you know where to look, and lingon (the red berries you get with the meatballs in the restaurant of a well known Swedish furniture store) are European cranberries. You had better ask your Mum or Dad what pear cider tastes like because it is much stronger today than when Bjarki drank it!

The Vikings never actually had horned helmets. That was something the Victorians attributed to them. So it is only in their 'cool clothes' that Bjarki and Alvi's hats had horns.

I hope this book has inspired you as much as the place names and the book 'The Saga of Asgard' inspired me when I first encountered them when I was young.

My Nana's Recipe for Scouse (Skaus)

Ingredients
1lb neck of lamb
4 or 5 carrots
1 medium turnip
2 large onions
2lbs potatoes
Salt and pepper
Water

Chop the meat up into approx 2cm squares. Peel and dice all the vegetables into 1-2 cm squares. Place it all in a big saucepan. Add water until it just covers the meat and veg. Season with salt and pepper. Bring it all to the boil stirring occasionally and then let it simmer until the potatoes, turnip and onions have fallen. It should be sloppily firm, not runny and not as dry as mashed potatoes. Serve with pickled red cabbage or beetroot.

You can use chicken instead of lamb or exclude the meat altogether for the veggie version, which is known as 'blind scouse'.

(PS. It *always* tastes better the next day!)

WHO'S WHO OF THE VIKING GODS IN THE PROLOGUE

Asgard – Home of the gods at the top of the World Tree of Life, Yggdrasill, a giant ash tree.

Odin – Chief god. He has only one eye having given the other to Mimir in exchange for the knowledge of everything. He had two ravens, and an eight legged horse called Sleipnr. Wednesday is named after Odin.

Thor – God of Thunder. Odin is his father and a giant was his mother. He uses his hammer, Mjolnir, to create storms. Thursday is named after Thor.

Frigg – Wife of Odin. Goddess of marriage and love.

Sif – Goddess of crops and fertility. Wife of Thor.

Balder – Son of Odin and Frigg. He is a handsome god and one of the best and wisest, despite his vanity. He returns from the dead after Ragnorok, the final battle, to rule Asgard.

Loki – The trickster god. Sly and sneaky and caused Balder's death, which was despised by the other gods.

Valkyries – An army of women formed by Odin to rescue those who fell in battle and bring them to Valhalla, the Hall of the Slain.

Mimir – Giver of wisdom and knowledge.

REFERENCES

'The Saga of Asgard' by Roger Lancelyn Green (published by Penguin Books, London 1960 and reissued in 1970 as 'Myths of the Norsemen').

'Scouse English' by Fred Fazakerley (published by Abson Books London 3rd edition 2003).

'Wirral and its Viking Heritage' by Paul Cavill, Stephen E Harding and Judith Jesch (published by English Place-Name Society, Nottingham 2000).

'Viking Mersey' by Stephen Harding (published by Countyvise Limited, Birkenhead 2002).

'Ingimund's Saga' by Stephen Harding (published by Countyvise Limited, Birkenhead 2006).

'Wirral Vikings' by Hrolf Douglasson (published by Countyvise Limited, Birkenhead 2005).

The Viking Alphabet or Futhark

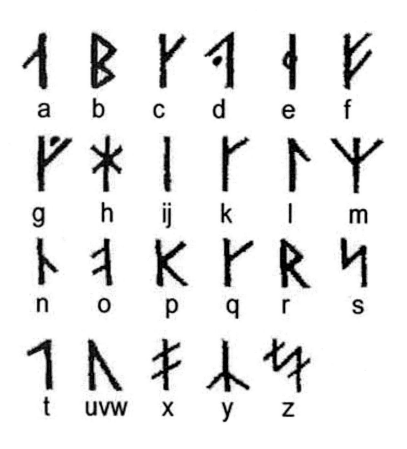